Dentists

A Level Three Reader

By Charnan Simon

Content Adviser: D. Milton Salzer, D.D.S.,
Editor, *Illinois Dental News*, Northbrook, Illinois

The Child's World®

Published by The Child's World®

P.O. Box 326
Chanhassen, MN 55317-0326
800-599-READ
www.childsworld.com

Photo Credits
© Ben Edwards/Tony Stone: 22
© Ed Wheeler/CORBIS: 21
© Jim Cummins/CORBIS: 3
© Kevin Laubacher/Taxi: 18
© Lee White/CORBIS: 17
© Mark Harmel/GettyImages: 10
© Royalty Free/CORBIS: cover, 5, 6, 9, 13, 14, 25, 29
© Tony Arruza/CORBIS: 26

Editorial Directions, Inc.: E. Russell Primm and Emily J. Dolbear, Editors;
Alice K. Flanagan, Photo Researcher

The Child's World®: Mary Berendes, Publishing Director

Library of Congress Cataloging-in-Publication Data
Simon, Charnan.
  Dentists / by Charnan Simon.
    p. cm. — (Wonder books)
Includes index.
Summary: An introduction to dentists and the work that they do.
  ISBN 1-56766-463-6 (lib. bd. : alk. paper)
  1. Dentistry—Juvenile literature. [1. Dentists. 2. Occupations. 3. Dentistry.]
I. Title. II. Series: Wonder books (Chanhassen, Minn.)
  RK63 .S566 2003
  531.14—dc21   2002151409

Have you been to the dentist
lately? Part of being a strong,
healthy person is having strong,
healthy teeth.

3

Dentists take care of our mouths. They make sure our teeth and **gums** stay healthy. Gums are the part of the mouth where teeth grow.

Brushing is good for your teeth and gums. →

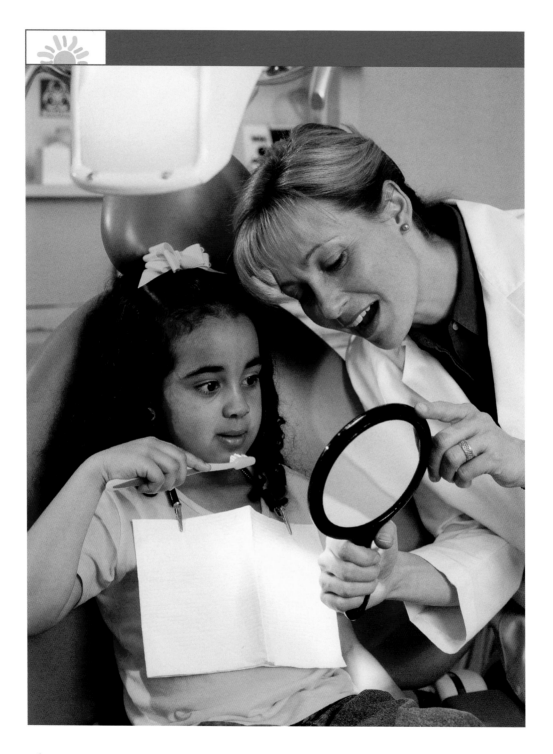

Dentists give people regular **checkups**. They clean teeth and make sure there are no problems. They teach people how to brush their teeth and use **floss**. They talk about foods that help build strong teeth.

← A girl learns how to brush her teeth.

Have you ever had a **cavity**? A cavity is a small hole in your tooth. Dentists fill up cavities. This helps keep your teeth strong—and your smile bright.

A dentist looks for cavities. →

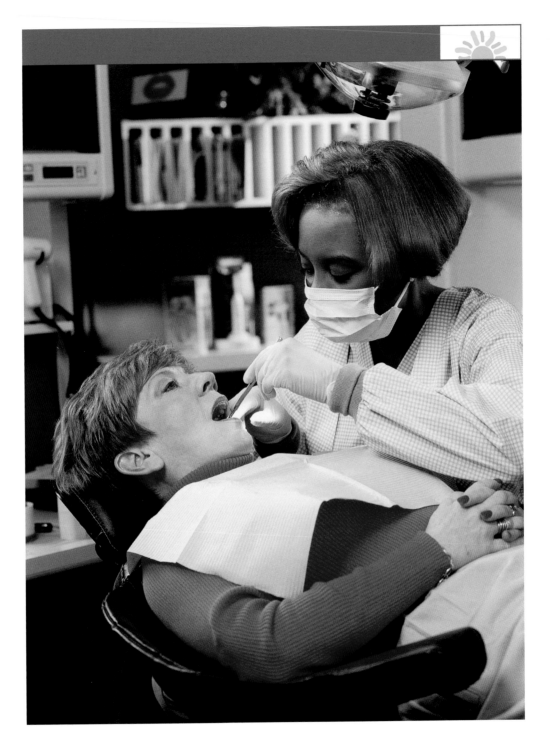

9

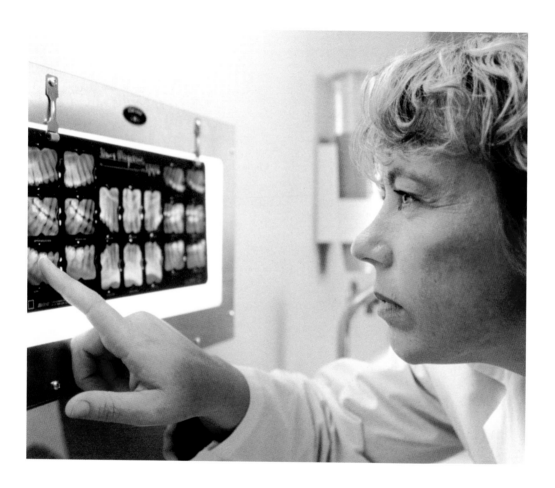

Dentists can tell a lot about teeth just by looking. But sometimes they need to know more. Then they take special pictures called **X rays**. These X rays let dentists see how your teeth are growing.

X rays show the roots of the teeth.

Sometimes teeth don't grow the right way. Sometimes teeth cause pain. When this happens, dentists may have to remove the bad tooth. They use special medicines and tools so it doesn't hurt.

A woman tells her dentist about the pain in her mouth. →

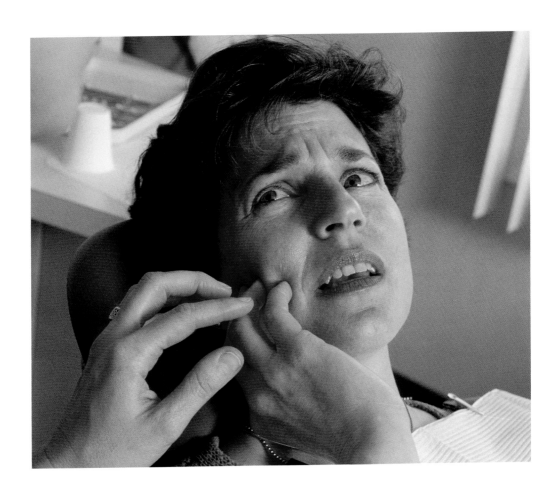

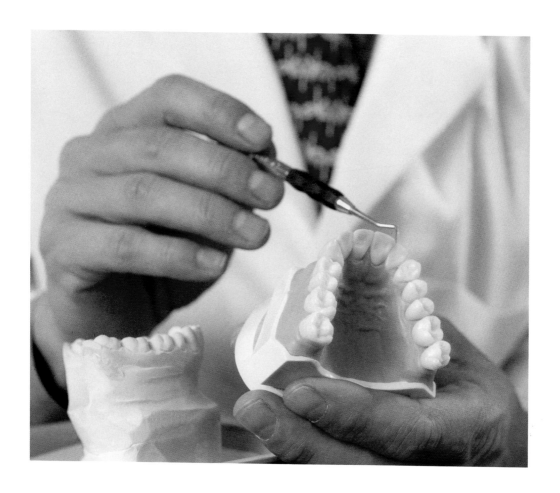

It takes a long time to become a dentist. First you have to study at a college or university. Then you have to study four more years at dental school. Some special dentists go on to study even longer.

A dental student examines a model of teeth.

One special kind of dentist is called an **orthodontist**. Orthodontists straighten out crooked teeth. They use braces, wires, and rubber bands to fix crowded or crooked teeth.

An orthodontist checks a girl's braces. →

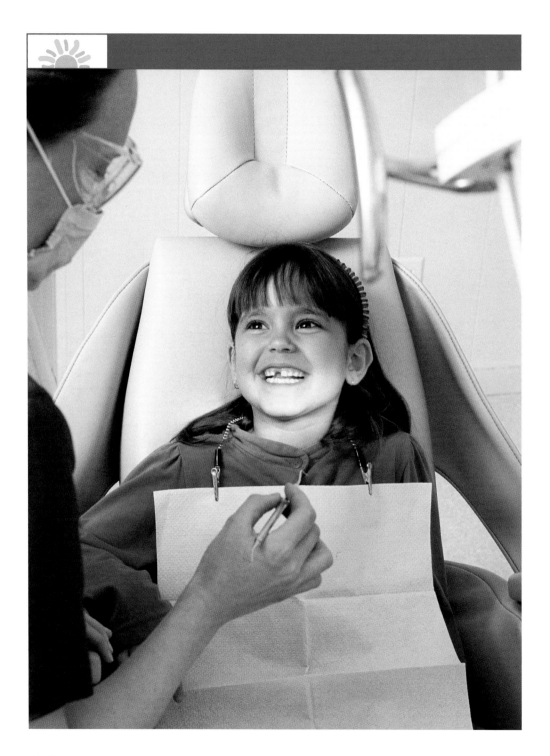

Dentists have to like teeth—and people! They must be good at solving problems and working with their hands. Sometimes people are nervous when they go to the dentist. A good dentist can help them relax and feel comfortable.

← A dentist makes her young patient smile!

Dentists are very careful not to spread **germs**. They often wear white or colored coats to keep things clean. They wear face masks and gloves. Dentists wash their hands many times every day.

This dentist wears a face mask and gloves. →

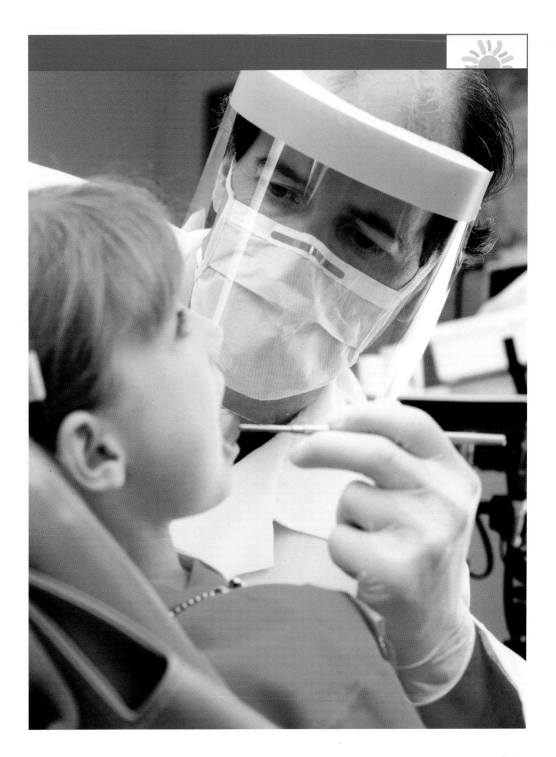

21

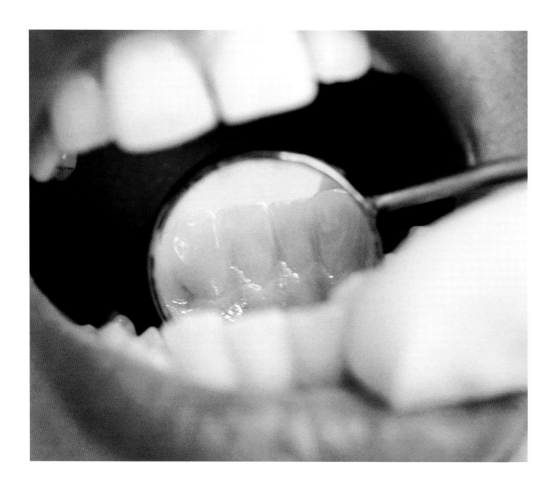

Dentists use many different tools. They use tiny brushes, **scrapers**, and mirrors. They have special chairs that go up and down. They have X-ray machines and bright lights that are easy to move.

Special mirrors help dentists see the teeth.

Sometimes people get their teeth knocked out in accidents. Sometimes people lose teeth as they get older. Dentists can make human-made teeth to replace them. Whew!

A dentist shows a model of teeth to a patient. →

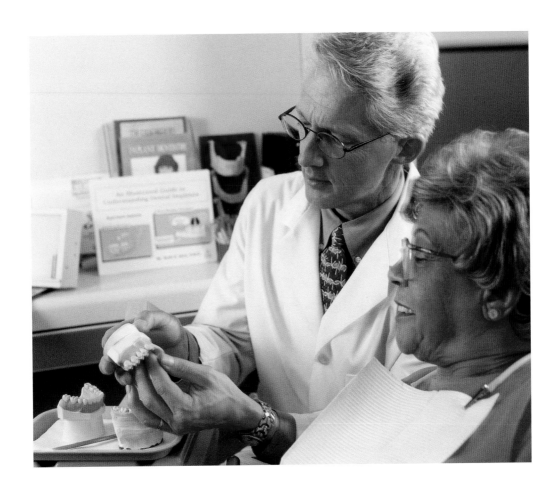

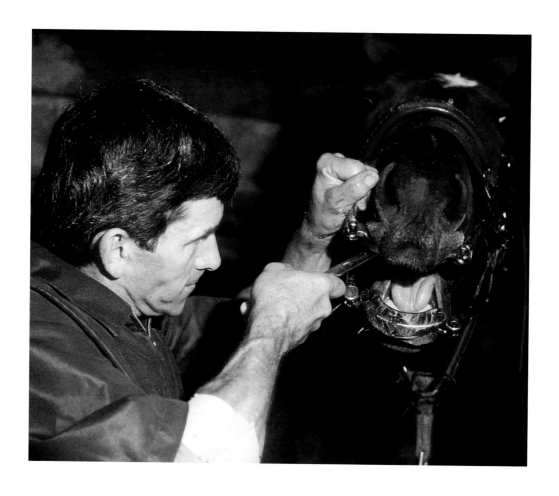

Not all dentists work in offices. Some dentists work in hospitals. Some dentists teach in dental schools. Some dentists even work in zoos. Animals can have toothaches, too!

← A dentist works on a horse's teeth!

Dentists take good care of our teeth. They also teach us how to care for our teeth between checkups. Being a dentist is something to smile about!

A dentist checks charts in his office. →

29

Glossary

cavity (KAV-ih-tee)
A cavity is a small spot or hole in a tooth. Cavities can weaken teeth if they are not filled in.

checkups (CHEK-uhpz)
Checkups are regular visits to a doctor or dentist to make sure you are healthy.

floss (FLAWSS)
Floss is a thin thread that people use to clean between their teeth.

germs (JURMS)
Germs are small living things that can cause disease.

gums (GUHMZ)
Gums are the areas of firm, pink skin where teeth grow.

orthodontist (or-thuh-DON-tist)
An orthodontist is a dentist who straightens crooked or crowded teeth.

scrapers (SKRAY-perz)
Dentists use scrapers to clean teeth.

X rays (EKS RAYZ)
An X ray is a special kind of picture that shows the inside of your body, including your teeth.

Index

To Find Out More

Books

Flanagan, Alice. *Dr. Kenner, Dentist with a Smile.* Danbury, Conn.: Children's Press, 1997.

Greene, Carol. *Dentists Care for Our Mouths.* Chanhassen, Minn.: The Child's World, 1998.

Keller, Laurie. *Open Wide: Tooth School Inside.* New York: Henry Holt, 2002.

Murkoff, Heidi. *What to Expect at the Dentist's Office.* New York: HarperCollins Children's Books, 2002.

Web Sites

Visit our homepage for lots of links about dentists:
http://www.childsworld.com/links.html

Note to Parents, Teachers, and Librarians:
We routinely verify our Web links to make sure they're safe, active sites—so encourage your readers to check them out!

Note to Parents and Educators

Welcome to Wonder Books®! These books provide text at three different levels for beginning readers to practice and strengthen their reading skills. Additionally, the use of nonfiction text provides readers the valuable opportunity to *read to learn*, not just to learn to read.

These leveled readers allow children to choose books at their level of reading confidence and performance. Nonfiction Level One books offer beginning readers simple language, word choice, and sentence structure as well as a word list. Nonfiction Level Two books feature slightly more difficult vocabulary, longer sentences, and longer total text. In the back of each Nonfiction Level Two book are an index and a list of books and Web sites for finding out more information. Nonfiction Level Three books continue to extend word choice and length of text. In the back of each Nonfiction Level Three book are a glossary, an index, and a list of books and Web sites for further research.

State and national standards in reading and language arts emphasize using nonfiction at all levels of reading development. Wonder Books® fill the historical void in nonfiction material for primary grade readers with the additional benefit of a leveled text.

About the Author

Charnan Simon lives in Madison, Wisconsin, with her husband and two daughters. She began her publishing career in the children's book division of Little, Brown and Company, and then became an editor of *Cricket Magazine*. Simon is currently a contributing editor for *Click Magazine* and an author with more than 40 books to her credit. When she is not busy writing, she enjoys reading, gardening, and spending time with her family.